my first golden book of abc's

an alphabet book

a

b

c

A GOLDEN BOOK · NEW YORK
Golden Books Publishing Company, Inc., New York, New York 10106

Created by Two-Can Publishing Ltd.
This edition copyright© 1999 Golden Books Publishing Company, Inc.
All rights reserved. Printed in Spain. No part of this publication may be reproduced or copied
in any form without written permission from the copyright owner.
GOLDEN BOOKS®, MY FIRST GOLDEN BOOK OF...®, G DESIGN™, and the distinctive spine are trademarks of
Golden Books Publishing Company, Inc.
Library of Congress Catalog Card number: 98-89664
ISBN: 0-307-45351-0 A MCMXCIX

Come along and join the fun. Learn your letters from A to Z. Look at the pictures and read the words. Test yourself with this simple picture puzzle.

a, b, c...

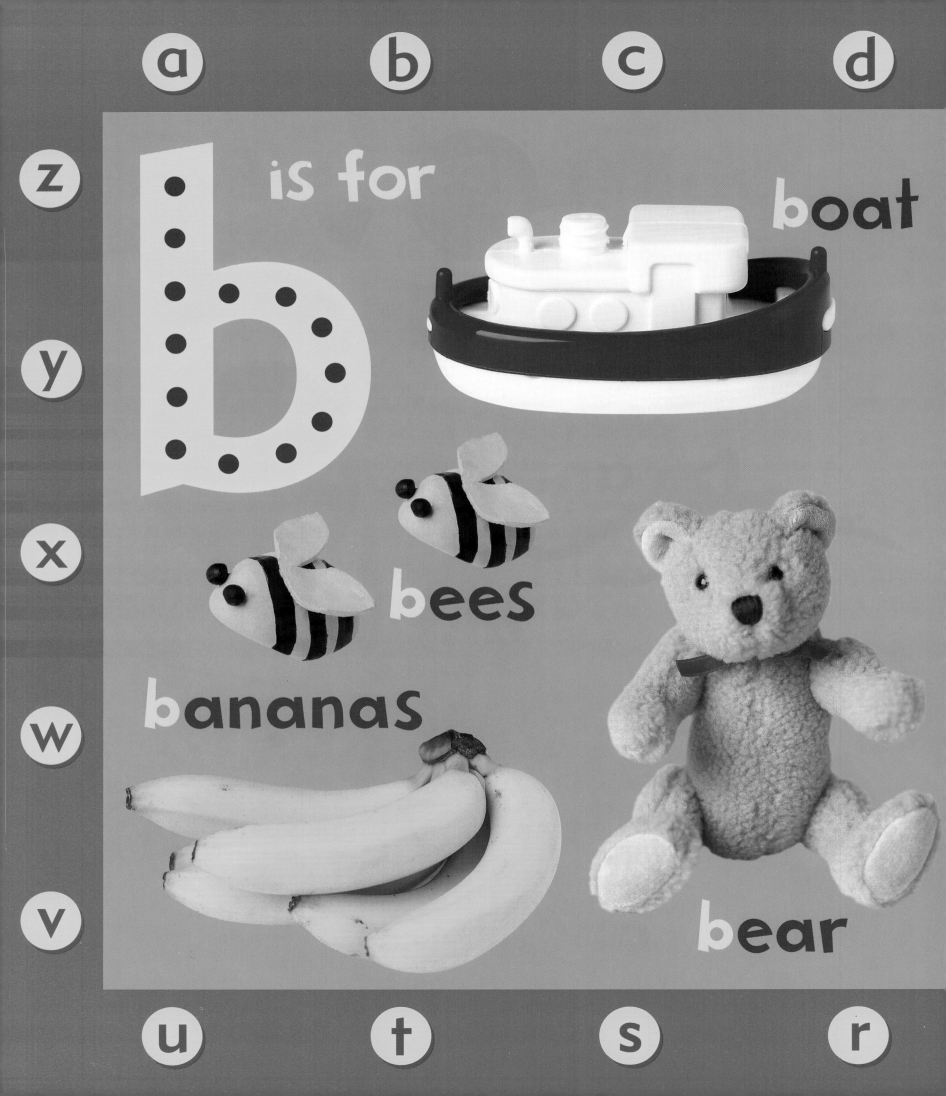

b is for

boat

bees

bananas

bear

blocks

bucket

balloon

butterfly

cookies

crayons

carrots

clock

cat

e f g h i j k l m q p o h

e   f   g   h

i

doll

j

dress

k

dominoes

l

dog

m

q   p   o   h

e is for

earrings

elephant

e f g h
i
j
k
l
envelope
egg
elf
m
q p o h

e
f
g
h
i
j
k
l
m
q
p
g
h

fish

flower

fairy

e f g h
i
j
k
giraffe
glass
gloves goat
l
m
q p o h

a b c d

z

y

x

w

v

u t s r

h is for

hippopotamus

house

horse

e   f   g   h

i

j

k

l

helicopter

hat

m

q   p   o   n

i is for

igloo

ice

ink

iron

K is for kite

king

l is for

ladybug

lamp

leaf

m is for

mouse

mop

money

mask

milk

moon

mug

monkey

e f g h i j k l m

q p o h

n is for

newspaper

nest

nails

necktie

e f g h

i

nuts

j

napkin

k

l

nurse

m

q p o h

O is for

orange

octopus

omelette

onion

otter

ostrich

owl

P is for

paper

picture

paints

pig

penguin

peas

pear

parrot

pizza

a b c d

z y x w v

q is for queen

u t s r

r is for

rabbit

robot

ruler

rattle

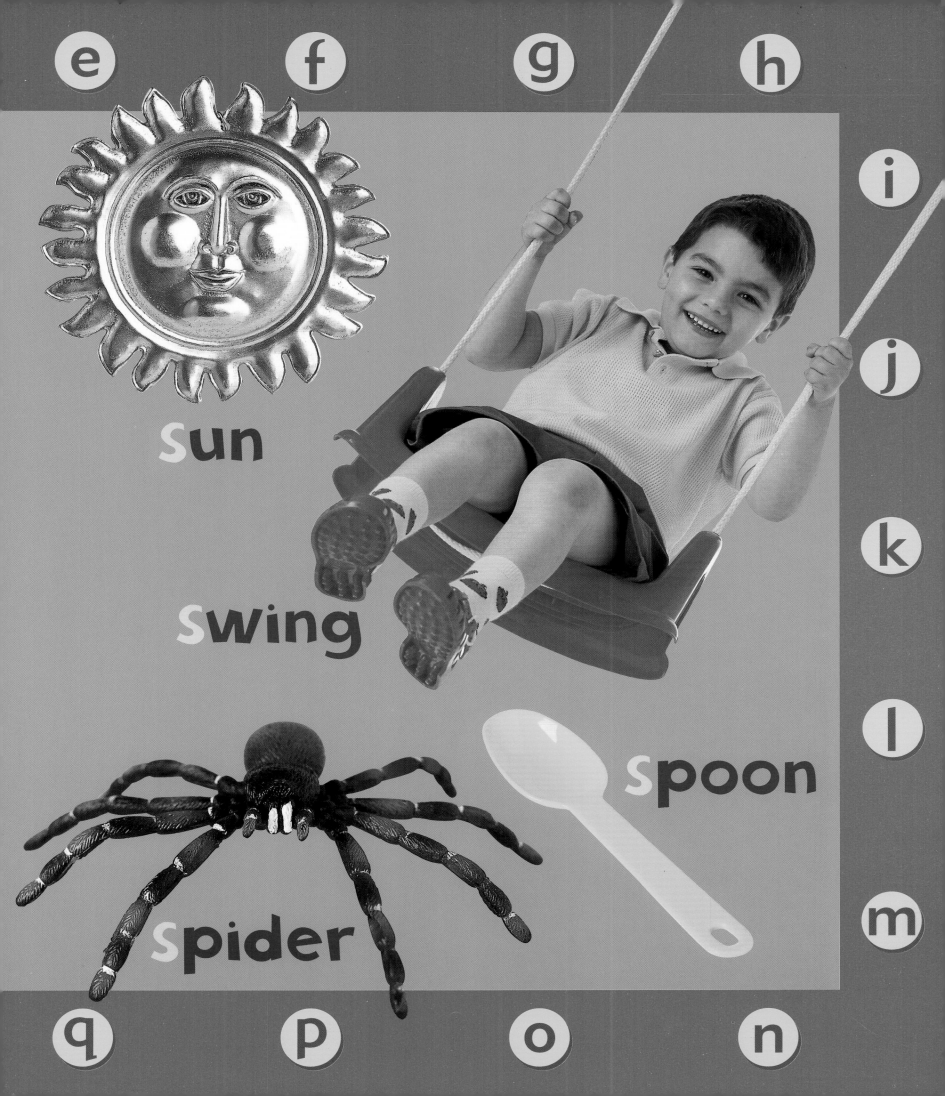

e f g h

i

j

sun

swing

k

l

spoon

spider

m

q p o n

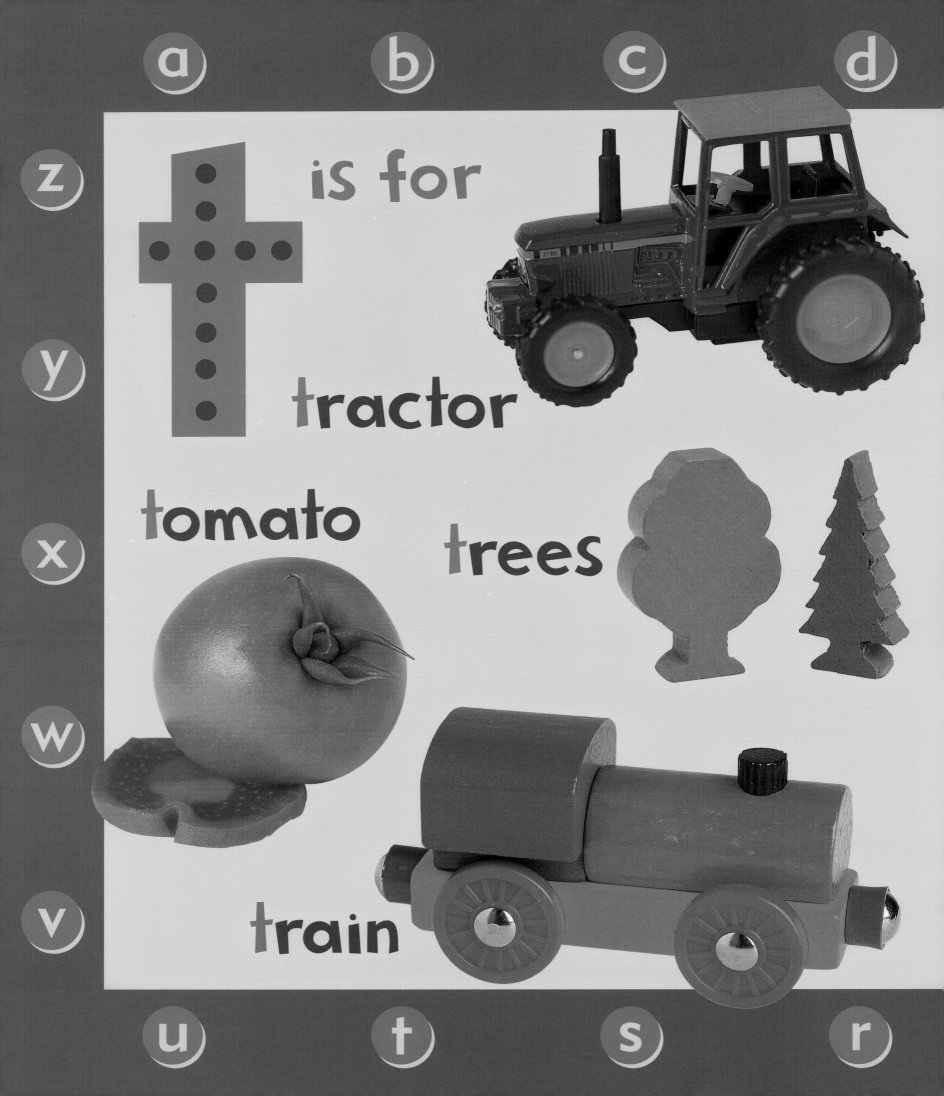

t is for

tractor

tomato

trees

train

e f g h

i

j

k

tiger

turkey

telephone

l

m

q p o n

U is for

umbrella

underwear

unicorn

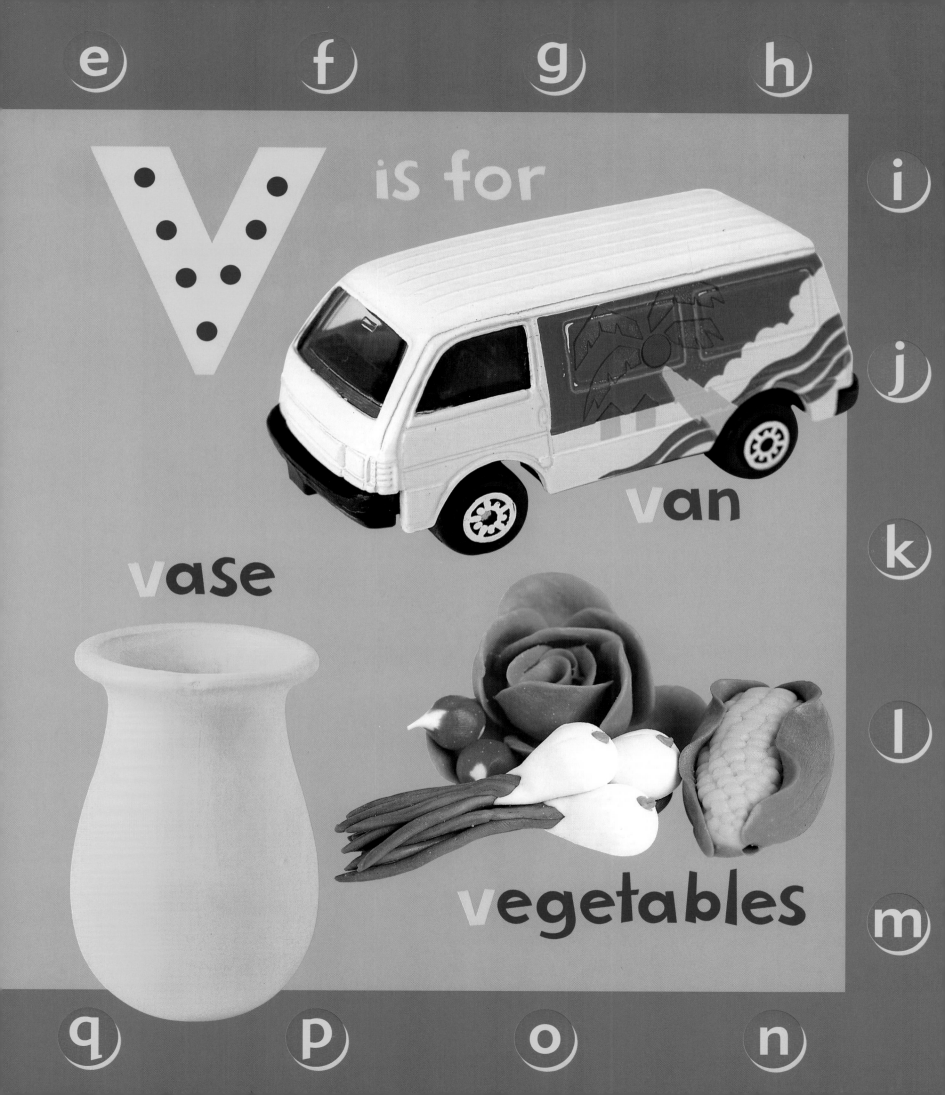

worm

whistle

watermelon

X is for
xylophone

Y is for
yarn
yo-yo

Z is for

zig-zag

zebra

zucchini

Can you name all the pictures? Point to

a b c d

z

y

x

w

v u t s r

Now that you know your ABC's,
you can come and play with me!
We'll start at A,
and go to Z.
It's really easy,
wait and see!